Cold Toast

Kathryn Aldridge-Morris

First published 2025 by Dahlia Books
ISBN 9781913624170

Copyright © Kathryn Aldridge-Morris 2025

The moral right of the authors has been asserted.

All rights reserved. No part of this publication may be reproduced, stored in or introduced into a retrieval system, or transmitted, in any form, or by any means (electronic, mechanical, photocopying, recording or otherwise) without the prior written permission of the publisher. Any person who does any unauthorized act in relation to this publication may be liable to criminal prosecution and civil claims for damages.

Printed and bound in the UK.

This book is sold subject to the condition that it shall not, by way of trade or otherwise, be lent, re-sold, hired out, or otherwise circulated without the publisher's prior consent in any form of binding or cover other than that in which it is published and without a similar condition including this condition being imposed on the subsequent purchaser.

A CIP catalogue record for this book is available from The British Library

For my mother, Wendy

Contents

These Boots Are Made for Walkin'	1
Double Lives	4
Yellow Straw, Red Straw	6
Cold Toast	7
Hotlines	9
Happiness is a Cigar Called Hamlet	11
Parasitos	12
Package Holiday: Monastir, All Inclusive	14
Perpetual War: 1983	16
Dinner Party Classic Recipe	18
Wall Space	19
To His Naked Eye	20
Raw Dough Rising	22
Electric Storm	24
Red Books	26
Stress	27
Roaring Twenties	29
While My Guitar Gently Weeps	30
The Last Message	32
Wine Tasting for Beginners	33
Girls Night Out	34

Undertow	36
Summer's Gone	39
When To Let Go	40
Trust the Process	42
Were You Ever There?	44
Elephant	45
Fogged Horizons	46
The Story You'll Never Tell	50

Acknowledgements
About the Author
About the Artist

These Boots Are Made for Walkin'
-after Tim Mara's *Portrait of Astrid, 1973*

If you were to ask anyone what sprung to mind about Astrid, it wouldn't be how she toured as part of a Pan's People cover troupe, or how she queued for hours to audition to be the next Bond girl, only to walk away last minute, feminist flyers stuffed into her handbag, arms linked with flame-haired Sheila the 'bra-burner' from Putney, or even how she hand-printed chapbooks of her freeform poetry, correcting the mistakes with nail varnish and selling them at Camden Market. It would be her boots. *Astrid?* they'd say. *Silver Boots Astrid?*

Because when she bought those silver platform boots, she wore them every day, whether it was behind the music counter at Woolworths where she worked weekends, or on one of the Women's Lib marches the men at The Anchor used to mock.

One boozy Friday night, Leo had asked the barman at The Anchor where he thought he might 'run into' the barmaid, Silver Boots Astrid. The next Saturday, Leo had presented himself at the cash desk with a picture disc edition of The Dark Side of the Moon and his work number.

Six months on, and Astrid was now gazing at a snow globe on top of her landlady's TV. Leo had brought it round for their half-year anniversary. Had it really been only six months? In return for setting her hair in rollers, the landlady let Astrid have use of the living room when her 'gentleman friend' came over. Recently, they'd sat through Citizen Kane and Leo—gorgeous Leo, like a perfected Ringo Starr— had provided commentary from the opening credits all the way through to when the snow globe slid out of Charles Kane's hand and shattered on the floor. He'd rambled on and Astrid had nodded and said she got it, and he'd rambled on some more, pouring himself wine and that was the first time she remembered thinking, *please don't ever leave your wife.*

How long would he stay this evening? She unzipped her boots and put his can of lager to her mouth. He was still on the payphone in the hall saying *But Bruce needs it for tomorrow,* saying *I know, darling, I know.* She swallowed the warm liquid. The three female figures suspended upside down in the snow globe were like defrosted human icicles; remnants of a man-made blizzard.

She turned on the TV for the Six O'clock news and the newsreader announced the police still hadn't caught the Saturday Night Strangler. He said that women and girls in and around Port Talbot should avoid going out at night. Astrid shook her head. How about the men stay in? She envisioned Sheila throwing a book at the TV. Bloody men! She reached for the ring pull Leo had tossed to the floor and twisted it onto her finger. He'd said he'd leave his wife and they could move to a New Town in Essex. He had never asked her if she *wanted* him to leave his wife. Or if she wanted to leave London. What would she do in Essex?

Astrid heard the clunk of the receiver and the flick of his lighter. She put the ring pull into the pocket of his green leather jacket on the back of her chair. Leo came back in and stood in front of the TV. The newsreader continued how the man they thought was the Strangler had an alibi, so they'd had to release him.

I've got myself a few hours, Leo said and winked. So sure of himself. Astrid motioned for him to get out of the way of the telly.

The suspect's wife had provided the alibi. Was she lying for him? But they'd found the van at the scene! And it was *the suspect's* van!

Astrid spotted Sheila outside striding towards her house. She held a box of pamphlets and was handing one to a neighbour. Maybe there was a Women's Lib meeting. The doorbell rang.

Ignore it, baby, said Leo, smoothing his moustache, smiling.

He picked up the snow globe and shook it with one hand. With the other, he took the cigarette from his mouth. Astrid saw the smoke curling from lips she still wanted to kiss, then looked at the plastic women, contained in their watery world, as the snow swirled prettily around their bodies. She zipped up her silver boots. And told him no, she wasn't going to ignore it.

Double Lives

I see Gwen at the school gates and she does this thing where she's looking but not seeing and I'm not in the mood so I wave my hands in her face and she says sorry, but she's still got this unseeing expression and I ask is everything okay? and she says yeah, if finding out your husband's living with another woman in the arse end of Wales is okay, and I say what, you mean your husband Rhys? and she nods, and says yes, my husband Rhys, and it's a crazy way for us to be carrying on because she only has one husband, but I'm not getting it, so I say Rhys Rhys? and she says, Rhys Rhys, and I feel a kind of vertigo because it was only last March when I noticed how he'd started hanging back after dropping the kids off, how easy it was to talk to him about all the stuff no one else ever wants to talk about, like how we all create our own prisons and how we'll bring our kids up to know there are more choices out there, how I was the only mother he spoke to, the only mother whose jokes he laughed at, and how good it felt to crack a crooked smile in the face Gwen always described as being like a slapped backside—and I think they've been together since they were fifteen, to be honest, I had thought a lot about that, about getting to your forties and only sleeping with one other person and if Rhys had ever thought about sleeping with other women before—before that first crazy time—and Gwen says she's going to get a test from the pharmacy because how many other women has he been sleeping with, and I'm like, you think there could have been *more?* and she shrugs, and I'm getting this weird double vision thing where the canopies on the horse chestnuts in front of us aren't lined up with the trunks and my left arm starts going numb, and I say, I'm not feeling too good and she says, Rhys told me you got migraines, and says, bye then, so I say, bye then, and watch her go; double-Gwen surrounded by an aura of fucked electrical impulses only I can see.

Yellow Straw, Red Straw

At some point, we'll forget the rabbit's name, how it came to die, the rush we were in to bury it, and when people ask, we'll shrug, and Vince will snarl his upper lip in the way his body's patterned to do since we went into care. But right now, we tip marbles and red and yellow plastic straws onto the kitchen floor of this latest house and lump Nibbles' body, still warm from the tumble dryer, into the Ker Plunk box. I fetch straw from his hutch and pack him in, nice and cosy. It's Vince's idea to bury him under the willow in the back garden, so we take an edge each and carry the Hasbro coffin into the chill autumn air. Vince digs a shallow grave with his scarred hands, and I lay the box in the earth. I give a short speech — you were a good rabbit, you never bit, etc etc — and Vince pulls a carrot from his back pocket and drops it in. Maybe it was that. The carrot. Maybe that was the moment when we just kinda knew we were good at this. Burying bodies. And killing things. Or maybe it was when we heard our foster mother scream and we ran back into the kitchen to find her lying on her back, legs akimbo like Woody in Toy Story, her head bleeding out over the marbles. In years to come they'll say we didn't kill her. They'll say you poor things, write about childhoods lost. They'll even say we didn't kill the rabbit. But right now, we know we've got to get rid of another body, the branches of the willow whisper us back and we've never felt so vital, so alive.

Cold Toast

In the seventies we become mothers. We buy brown curtains and burnt-orange sofas and make homes for husbands who don't come home at night. We make toast and marmalade and set the table and we get the kids ready for school. We put Clubs and Kit Kats and Wagon Wheels and white bread sandwiches in Tupperware lunchboxes. We have cream rotary telephones and pop-up telephone directories with our girlfriends' names. Our phones ring sometimes in the night. Always during the day. In the seventies we answer the phone and say *648-9938 HELLO?* or whatever number it is—so many things we can't forget. We hear the breath of other women on the other end, and we move the magnifying slider from A-Z, each letter popping up a new possibility. We call Speaking Clock to hear another adult voice, to know we're not going mad: the kids *are* late for school, our husbands *are* late back from their shifts, their picket lines, their liquid lunches. The Speaking Clock tells us *it is eight twenty-five and thirty-six seconds*. We call back, and the Speaking Clock tells us *it is eight twenty-five and fifty-five seconds*. We pack the kids off to school and our phones ring again when the house is empty, and we let them ring. We sit with our husband's toast and write up our study notes from Open University courses aired at two in the morning. We learn about psychology and sociology and all the ologies we never dreamt we'd be good at before we got jobs at Lewis's, Woolworths, and C&A. When our husbands come back with just enough time to shower and change into new shirts, we cry and we scream, *What time do you call this?* and they ask if we've had our Valium, prise our arms from their waists and go again.

In the seventies, we eat cold toast, we call the Speaking Clock, and we wait for our time.

Hotlines

When I was ten, the first thing I did after school every day was go to the red telephone box a mile from my house and listen to the voice of the Yorkshire Ripper. His was a northern voice, flat, and other. *Getting desperate*, Mum said when the police released a recording of his calls to them, and she told us to quiet while she scribbled the number on the back of a cereal packet. The head of the police was called George, and Jack always started out by saying, *Hello, I'm Jack* and then speaking straight to George, asking him if he was stupid or something. I thought George probably looked like Columbo and was doing the stupid thing on purpose.

At home the phone rang all the time. Mum wouldn't let us pick up. When she was in the bath or late back from work, I'd lie on the orange, foam sofa, *Hart to Hart* turned low, waiting for the calls to start. They always did. I'd grab the receiver before it rang twice. There was never anyone there. Just a crackling like a broken telly. And breathing. Soft and northern. *Jack?* I asked. If he was clever enough to get George's number, he could get mine. If he was clever enough to kill ten women, then he could just as easily kill a goofy kid who was bottom at running.

Jack spoke for about two minutes. It was called 'Dial-the-Ripper' hotline. All anyone was talking about was the Yorkshire Ripper. They said on the news that girls weren't going out in Yorkshire anymore. Girls meant women too. The newspapers ran full-page ads and both billboards on the High Street had police posters with: FLUSH HIM OUT. HE DOESN'T DESERVE YOUR PITY.

I was good at listening in on phone calls. It was just a case of picking up the exact same time as Mum and then staying dead quiet. *Bloody Coral*, Mum always said to her friends, *I know he's with her*. And I thought of Dad swimming through an exotic coral reef with a garland round his neck like *Hawaii Five-O*. Next thing Mum's behind me screaming do I know what happens to little girls who don't know when to mind their own business.

George did get clever but not in the way he hoped. They did a DNA test on the saliva of one of Jack's envelopes. Turned out the man calling was just some alcoholic hoaxer from Sunderland. *Another one who doesn't know when to stop*, said Mum. They put him in prison and the hotlines stopped. I asked mum if I could have Dad's number, now he was living with Coral. She wrote it on the back of the cereal box, ripped it off and told me to keep it.

Happiness is a Cigar Called Hamlet

Loneliness is as dangerous as fifteen cigarettes a day. My mother doesn't smoke, so I steal cigarettes from the purses of my father's girlfriends. Let the unlit filters stick to my tongue. My father smokes Hamlet cigars. Happiness is a cigar called Hamlet, runs the ads. Divorce is like sugar in the late seventies. Men get a taste for it. My dad gets a taste for it. He leaves us with the contrails of tobacco leaf in our hair. Takes his happiness with him. Leaves us skint. Leaves us teeth-yellowed from the sugar with which our mother coats his absence. Too busy chewing to ask where he is. She wants to treat us. Her fatherless kids watching the Flintstones. Stone-age kids with dads and pet dinosaurs and other stuff we'll never have. My mother writes in tiny diaries the size of a candy cigarette pack. When she dies of cancer decades later, I'll find one of these doll-sized diaries. I'll see how she compressed the wood-smoked words *saw no one spoke to no one* across the windows of a whole week. And then another. See how the paper, thin as skin at the end of life, see how it curls like the tip of a lit cigarette.

Parasitos

We buy the house as a quick sale from the school nit nurse. I sense them the second we set foot inside. Parasites. Hunting for scalp.

Why did *we* have to move here?

I become convinced the pine wood panelling on the living room walls is riddled with ticking termites. Not just the walls. The wooden floors too, the tiles slotted together; the entire room a mind-puzzle, seen from the inside out.

Sitting on the foam sofa, with its worn orange cover, I tuck my feet under to stop the nurse's leftover lice licking my toes, hopping up my thighs, moon-landing on my head, while the grain of the wood swirls with its invisible, predatory life force. Nothing seems stable, least of all the walls holding up this latest roof over our heads.

I take to wearing sunglasses in the house. On account of the vertigo from the lines. Vertical lines down the panelling. Jigsaw lines on the floor. Horizontal lines from the blinds across the square bay window, one chink in the metal slats, from that time someone threw a Rubik's cube. The only breach in the symmetry.

The evenings get darker, earlier. I peer out into the orange rush hour, scratching, restless, breathing in the dust, waiting. When you get home, you sit me down. Gently remove my ear defenders. It's important. What you need to tell me. He's coming back. We're all going to try again.

You tell me straight in one long line so there's nothing to read between. I twitch. Nod. What else can I do? The room is silent just long enough for me to tell you I think another wall panel has been eaten away.

Package Holiday: Monastir, All Inclusive

She wants to go back up to the room, like the other families hours ago, but her father's holding court at the poolside bar and beckoning a group of men in yellow oilskins, dragging their boat ashore, humping their catch onto the sand. Now is when the locals working night shifts stop by the beachside hotels, as the tourists sleep on sheets stained with sun oil, alarm clocks set early to bring towels down to stake loungers.

'I'll get a round in!' her father shouts. He can fraternize with anyone – that's his forté: banter with the working classes comes as easy as greasing top brass. It's a people-person prowess you've either got or you haven't.

The fishermen don't know what he's saying, this rubberneck in tennis whites, burnt salmon-pink from the forehead down, drinking with his daughter – how old, twelve, thirteen? – in her tiny shorts, legs white as squid. But they understand the tray with shot glasses and join him.

She wanders to the far side of the swimming pool beside the beach, next to the crates of gutted, dead fish. How they must have flopped and gasped in those men's gloved hands only minutes earlier. Her father calls her and she shivers in the warm night air. She can't see where the sea ends and the sky begins and how bottomless the world seems right now. She doesn't want to be talking to old men at four in the morning. She wants to go to bed.

'He'll take us out on the boat,' says her father, his arm round the shoulders of one of the men. 'If you give him a kiss.'

'What?' she asks. She laughs because she's scared. And he laughs because: Don't Spoil This.

He repeats it, this time an edge to his voice. Like when they'll be driving back from the airport to her mother's house, and the car veers, bumping over cats eyes as she says she'll never go away with him again. The kind of edge that says: stay in line.

She looks to the bar for help. Maybe the lifeguard who helped on that first day when her father drifted out to sea on an inflatable donut? Or the cleaner who'd knocked at midday, found him sleeping, still in fancy dress on the bathroom floor, and stroked her hair, 'Habibi,' she'd said.

But there is no-one.

Her father's new friend leans in, white eyebrows thick and wild. He smells of snapper. His lips, thin as fish-wire, open. Her body flops as his beard nets her mouth and he works his tongue like a knife prising open a clam. Tomorrow they'll go on the boat and her father will wear yellow oilskins and hook a tuna and pronounce it the best day yet.

Perpetual War: 1983

If anyone had come looking, they'd have found me at the local library after school. The smell of loop pile carpet tiles would come to trigger the visceral joy I got from reading *Mandy for Girls* in decades to come. *Mandy*. Stories of orphans, stepmothers, events beyond control. Between the Thursdays when *Mandy* came out, I lay behind the splintered, rosewood comic rack and pulled out the closest books within reach. It was there I found Orwell. *Animal Farm* at first. Then *1984*. Nothing in *Mandy* had prepared me for 1984.

My mother warned me not to read it. Didn't I get enough nightmares? It was true I dreamt of poltergeists and disappearing family members and the fear was starting to pool in mottled marks under my skin. But still. I read it, over and over, devouring the dystopia with the same self-destructive fervour with which I got through packs of Kings candy cigarettes.

I saw Big Brother in the Ford Cortina that would pull up outside our house at night, keep the engine running, watching. I heard Big Brother on the end of the phone, me stretching the yellow coiled wire, wrapping it round and round my fingers, listening to a black and white breath. I started to notice how it was only me and Mum who got the calls from Big Brother. I kept a diary. I wondered if Dad was involved. I was sure I saw him climb out of the Cortina one time.

My parents forbade me from watching the film the night it was scheduled to air. I was a nervous wreck already, they said. Look at the eczema, the tic in my right eye. But I snuck out from my room, tiptoed downstairs to Oceania and crouched behind the orange foam sofa watching Winston and the rats, the breaking of a human being, the betrayal of a woman. *Do it to Julia! Not me! Do it to her!* Watching this man doing whatever it took to look after number one. Then with my small body clenched, I crept back to bed, through the blinking of headlights in the hallway.

Not before seeing the phone receiver ripped and dislocated, moaning from the floor, alongside a shattered glass and the dent in the chair where Dad usually sat.

Dinner Party Classic Recipe
(From 'Cooking For You')

1. Line the dinner table with seven full wine glasses — one extra-large, for your husband.
2. Stick The Mamas and The Papas on your new Fidelity record player. Using a spatula, place old friends in allocated seats and mix until soft and creamy, gradually beating in The Carpenters.
3. Slowly whisk up a little small talk with your husband's new colleague. The one with smoky eyes helping herself to Blue Nun and popping Valium from a blister pack.
4. Remove colleague— dabbing her eyes with her kaftan sleeve, as your husband flirts with your best friend— and place in preheated lavatory, spacing yourselves well apart.
5. Carefully spoon out your words: Stop. The. Calls.
6. Now flatten her with a fork.
7. Bring out colleague and place on a wire rack at the centre of attention.
8. Shower her with edible pink hearts and finely drizzle the lie he's never brought home a colleague before.
9. Leave to cool before serving, as will crumble easily while still warm.

Wall Space

Sure, I was a screensaver, but otherwise, it was photos of *her* kids round Dad's house. Sharon and Darren. At the zoo, the mall, the beach. Dad buried in sand, a Budweiser cock, eyes scrunched with laughing, or sand, or whatever other jokes they had.

Wait, I'm wrong. There *was* one of me downstairs—over the TV— all eighties perm and hormones. One weekend visit it vanished. A dog certificate in its place.

'You don't even have a dog,' I said to her.

She stroked my head. 'No honey,' she said. 'But if we did? That's the dog we'd have.'

To His Naked Eye

At eleven, I spend most of my time at Helen's, sunk in a stained leather sofa, the lounge lit by a crack in the curtains drawn against daylight, the blue shaft of second-hand smoke from her mother like a cinema projector. We're watching Texas Chainsaw Massacre, Carrie, The Exorcist. Her mother lets us do this because she's past the giving-a-shit stage of parenting; Helen's brothers being grown up, unemployed, and upstairs stamping to The Jam, while we're in the dark, considering puberty, wondering if that head spinning's a thing we need to worry about.

One day Helen's brother Guy comes out of his bedroom. He doesn't slam into the lounge, pointing at my brown cords asking, 'What the fuck are you wearing?' as usual. He comes in and says, 'Hello.' I don't reply because I still don't want, nor know, how to talk to boys and I'm not sure I'm ready to handle their level of banter yet. Guy's decided he wants to be a professional photographer and because there's fuck all else to photograph, he'll photograph the pair of us idiots. Tells me to sit on a chair. I'm to be McCartney and should put my arms into a V-shape. Helen's Lennon. She stands behind me and rests her chin on my head. He takes some shots then disappears into his bedroom, converted into a darkroom by hanging dirty towels in the windows.

Helen's mother comes for her ciggies. Asks if we want a cup of tea. She always makes a comment about me taking sugar which hurts, I don't know why. Who has sugar in their tea? she asks. And I add that to my list of not knowing how to be in the world. Thinking about the photos makes my stomach bloat like I've eaten too many sugared fangs. Helen's mum inhales then blows smoke rings at the cat. I imagine Guy stirring and developing images of me, my face floating in his liquid chemicals, the gelatine layer of the paper swelling as the perm I cried about for three days becomes visible.

Guy kicks open the door. Grins. He's pleased with himself and the photos he's pegged up. We're to go and look. I shrug, say I've got to go back for tea. He dashes off to get the photo, brings it back, says something about next time, and cool isn't it, but I hear only the jibes I'm sure he's going to make the moment I'm gone. I don't get to see my McCartney. I slam out, with my fur-lined hood pulled over my head, terrified he can see it spinning.

Raw Dough Rising

Whatever happened for her mother to stick the rolling pin under her pillow? An axe-wielding stranger? Body-snatcher at the foot of her bed? Who knows, but at some point, it rolled its way out of the kitchen for good.

'Doesn't your mother ever bake anymore?' asks her father one visit, the house swelling with the male scent of nylon socks. She shrugs and scrambles upstairs to make the beds before her mother gets home from the library, plumping the pillows and straightening the rolling pin.

'I'll get my Pattie to bake you one of her epic puff pastry cakes,' her father says when she comes back down. He throws himself onto the sofa and she stares at the sweat-patched soles of his feet, trying to conjure the smell of her mother's own shortcrust pastry. She recalls the scalloped cookie cutters she'd used: three heart-shaped cutters they were.

His visits peter out. His tyres are slashed one week, then he calls to say there's been another attack on a prostitute and the street's sealed off. Next, he's lost his keys.

'I've had enough,' says her mother. She drives her daughter over and drops her at the stairwell of his tower block. Her father's flat smells different. Cherries and cake. Pattie waves her in like she already owns the place. The furniture's been rearranged, and she wants to tell her mother there are no books. She'd learnt from her that's all you need to know about a person.

'Her mother's never in the kitchen,' says her father, untying the knot of Pattie's apron. Pattie giggles, flours the wooden kitchen top and his daughter watches as she rolls and flattens, rolls and flattens. They shuffle into his bedroom as Pattie's puff cake bakes, its silhouette rising behind the steamed oven window. When did her mother last giggle? Last smile? She twists the oven knob to the max and stuffs Pattie's rolling pin into her bag. She's ten. Old enough to make her own way home in the dark.

Electric Storm

It's been twenty minutes since the first bolt of lightning ripped a scar through the purple night sky. Since my mother said to swim in the rain — it's fun. Since her boyfriend Colin said he'd join us— to check we're okay. She'd shrugged off the kiss he tried to burrow in her neck, lit a cigarette and sat on the deck. She wanted to stay; watch the storm from the villa, watch the rain roll in from across the Loire.

The water is eel-black. I swim close to the pool floor, broken tiles rubbing against my belly. A burst of white and I see everything: dead mosquitoes on the surface, my sister's arms propelling, and a man's naked body standing in the deep end. I stop moving, count twenty and thunder vibrates through the water. When I surface, we're in blackness again, other than a solitary pool light that flickers to my left.

Your mum's right, shouts Colin. This *is* fun.

Yeah, I say, and see my sister's silhouette on the pool steps.

Too many bugs, she says and heads back to the villa, her feet slapping quickly on the wet stone, the way little kids' feet do.

You know the Bridge Your Legs game? calls Colin. Lightning flashes the poolside white and I see my flip-flops in the stiff grass and Colin's clothes flung over a lounger bent in on itself.

I dip back below the surface and swim towards his legs. The contours fizz as his knees straighten. Under the water, the thunder rumbles like a bedsheet shaken. My fingertips brush his thighs. I tilt my hands against the flow of the water. Push ahead. His leg muscles close around my waist, clench, long enough to count two. He lets go. A cloud of blinding white light explodes overhead and from underwater I hear him shouting the storm's right on top of us, could strike him any minute. Him being the highest thing around.

Red Books

In the nineties we get our first jobs, recession jobs, as drivers and carers, jobs in bookshops selling Marxist books and books by writers who've driven from communist states in lime green Ladas, their books boxed and hidden in car boots; and after shelving the books and selling some of the books, after this thing we call work at the time, we drink; we drink two for the price of one, four for the price of two and when happy hour becomes happy night, eight for the price of four; we drink work nights and we work hungover; we get to work late and we jump off the Tube one stop early to stoop in alleys and clear the slate for the evening to come; then we work the cash tills and pack books and smoke fags with our late morning coffee, think about hairs of dogs and stare out at the dogs tied to bike racks, empty besides the dogs and the bikes of the students; students who buy our books in their breaks and smoke in the shop and dream in the shop, dream of what they'll be in the world, once they've read all the books on the shelves we now stack, having read all the books on the shelves in the eighties.

Stress

Dying is a full-time job. There's so much to do before the formal diagnosis of what you're dying from: blood tests, X-rays, scans and cardiograms, bone marrow biopsies and, for good measure, emergency blood transfusions.

Mum doesn't say anything. We're in a portacabin in the hospital car park because parts of the Victorian main building are being refurbished. What this means, we'll soon discover for ourselves, is that local artists are painting supersized flower heads along the corridor walls. We'll spend months of Mum's remaining life staring at metre high stigmas and stamen, wondering who thought gargantuan yellow stigma would make anyone feel better. But for now, we imagine magnolia and wards full of people not us.

Rain plothers down on the steel roof. 'I didn't bring my umbrella,' says Mum.

The consultant looks up at the ceiling. Frowns. We all look up. 'It's heavy,' he confirms. Now the auxiliary nurse is nervous, checking her bag under her chair.

'I've got an umbrella, Mum,' I say, but she says, 'Shush.'

'First up, a skélétal scan,' says the consultant.

'A *skélétal* scan?' I ask and Mum gives me one of her looks. In years to come, I'll catch myself missing those looks, her abrasive thanks, even the silences. It will shake me.

'A skelétal scan, yes,' he says.

'*Is* that where the syllable falls on skeletal?' I ask.

'For god's sake,' says Mum, and he says, 'That's okay. I think we're done for now.'

We go to the counter for scans and they give us a map and a ticket and it's the same kind of ticket they use for raffles. I don't make this observation out loud though, I say, 'Mum, he got the syllable wrong. He got it wrong.' She nods and we exit into the rain.

Roaring Twenties

She remembers the vodka-clear starts of nights. Leggings, suede jackets and crimping hair, her sister separating strands. Rainy platforms, ring-pulls and beer the colour of old blood, trains that curve through mizzle from the suburbs into the London light, the punch of hot noise when the pubs doors open. Bands on makeshift stages, Monkey boots, dancing and not giving a shit, bouncers, the midnight rain straightening her hair, the closest pubs a short run away, fragments – *a beautician, right? – treading a thin line – a lot to learn—* the guitarists, the drummers, the strange yet familiar smell of men's duvets, the sound of their flatmates splashing water, doors slamming, unshaven chins between her breasts, the taste of kebabs, egg rice, ready lasagnes from the night before at 4 in the morning, bechamel sauce at the back her throat, the way they pull on their jeans no pants, don't offer coffee, call her anything but her name, and her, lying there, naked: not remembering, not remembering a damn thing.

While My Guitar Gently Weeps

Four months to the day after George Harrison died, Ron was barbecuing Cumberland sausages at the back of his terraced house, wearing nothing but extra-large boxers and a rubber apron. Fat grease shone on his chest hair.

'Local paparazzi's been,' he said, snapping open a can of Fosters.

'Yeah?' His daughter pretended not to remember.

'For an interview. They took my photo.' He poured twiglets into a cut glass goblet. 'I had to look sad.'

'Obviously.'

'It's not my best face and I'm going to be on the front cover.'

It had been thirty minutes, but it was no use — Pepsi wasn't going to cut it. 'Go on then, Dad. Pass me a beer.'

'Everything in life's the sum of all that went before it.'

'What you're essentially saying is that if it wasn't for you, the Beatles wouldn't —'

'What I'm essentially saying is that George Harrison was lucky he went to my school. Harry's kid needs a guitar, your Nan said, and that was it. I never practised — though I was told I had talent — so George got mine for three pounds and ten shillings.'

He paused to turn a sausage. 'But I mean what eleven-year-old practises guitar?'

'George Harrison?'

He spun round with his tongs, brown sauce whipping the air like a cable, and crooned into them. Happier than he'd been in a long time. Like *really* happy. He stopped to light a Hamlet cigar.

'Not bad what he achieved though. Son of a bus driver from the backstreets of Liverpool,' she said, recalling how her mother had had to stop studying to take on more hours at Littlewoods after he left.

Ron mic-dropped his tongs onto the Realgroove decking. 'And where did it get him, hey? All that success? Where did it get him?'

She drank deeply. Nothing else to do. Lips round that steel tear-shaped hole in a tin.

'Where *did* it get him, dad? You tell me.'

'George Harrison is dead. John Lennon is dead.' He reached for a fork. 'Me? Still here. Still barbecuing.' Then, with the sound a knee makes when it pops, he pierced the seal of a burger pack, straight through the *Sell-By Date* he'd neglected to remove.

The Last Message

You tell her how angry you are at the traffic on the way in, the parking meters all bust, the parking spots all time-restricted, the rotating doors, the lift that always has to go down before it goes up, the officious nurse who took the flowers, the weather too damn hot for April, the chair that you're sitting on — has it even been wiped down? — the heat in the ward, the food on her tray; *Slops in custard*, she says, *You always hated custard*, then holds out her arm – they can never find her veins, and in days how you'll wish you took her hand, but right now you can't see a way round the blood-black bruising so she says she's angry too; the windows don't open, the noise at night, how the black outside seems to bleed into the room, the constant beeping, the beep of the saline drip, the beep of the heart monitor, then between the beeping the silence; the silence of someone else's blood circulating around her body.

Driving home you pull over, take out your phone, there are things to say, urgent things, one of those things being how she's wrong: you *don't* hate bloody custard, never have – why would she even think that? — you *loved* the Bird's custard she served every night of the week. Was it your fault they stopped eating it? But a warden has appeared and he's saying, *you can't park here, move along, you can't just pull over in a no-waiting area*, so there's no time for custard, instead you text TRAFFIC WARDENS! then pull out, cursing through your closed window, glancing in the rear-view mirror as the hospital fades away.

Wine Tasting for Beginners

You smirk as the waiter pours a dash of the red for you to taste because a drink's a drink, but your date seems to like the show of it all, so you enter Act 1 and swirl and sip and sure, the plums cloy, tannins stick to your teeth and you suss how this bottle will end—hungover in bed with another Sauvignon Dom—but it'll be years before you learn to taste with your nose and trust your first sip, say no, send it back; years before you learn you can do so much better than drink wine that's corked.

Girls Night Out

Suppose this man with his sovereign ring doesn't punch you square in the face, and the bridge of your nose — pierced only Wednesday on a whim for your twentieth birthday —doesn't pop like a champagne cork, your blood Jackson Pollock the ground.

Suppose you've not burst from the bar onto Clapham High Street, like a Catherine Wheel spinning with all the good shit that's aligned all at once just for you; party streamers stuck to your Monkey boots, the dye from the crepe paper leaching red on the puddled pavement. He hasn't leant himself up against the bus shelter, pulled out his cock, started pissing on the plastic seats. And you — high and happy and invincible with your nose stud and new friends and it's raining men hallelujah.

Suppose he doesn't need to know oi who you looking at? and it hasn't been only six months since you dropped dry soil from clenched fists onto your boss's coffin and left the cemetery with a bounce in your formal black pumps, swore to never be afraid again.

And suppose when you see Sovereign Man for the last time—his mates slapping him on the back, *nice one mate* — it's through the window of a vehicle with an orange light, not blue, not flashing, and the driver doesn't ask about your blood group, he wants to talk about the price of petrol and how it's all gone to the dogs, how this job will be the death of him, the violence, the fighting, not just the boys but the girls and how you wouldn't understand. And you twiddle your nose stud and rest your head against the cab window, and on the street there are women dancing and partying, and looking wherever it suits them.

Undertow

Dad and I are the first to try the lock gates on the canal after the long winter, and our small hire boat bobs against the jetty as we survey the debris: a season's worth of spooled junk, man-made and natural. We stare into the canal from the towpath— two helpless academics hoping if we think about it hard enough a solution will froth up between the branches, beer bottles and petrol cans. I hand him the lock key before he decides to bail. There's a pub not a hundred yards from here.

'How would I know how to use this?' he asks.

'Just have a go. Have a bit of fun with it.'

'Fun?' he says. 'Did you know the etymology of 'fun' is to cheat or to trick a person?'

I wait for him to repeat himself, as is the wont of professors.

'The etymology is to —'

'—cheat or trick, I say. 'I heard you the first time.'

When I catch myself repeating stuff at home, Bruno will stroke my arm. 'Honey, you're not like him,' he'll say. But I've only been in post a year.

Dad makes as though the lock key has slipped from his hand and the heavy steel clunks onto the towpath. He strides over to the Visitors' Board. 'Why we didn't just meet at The Drunken Duck, I'll never know,' he says.

I grab the lock key and fix it to the spindle. As I wind it, the gritted teeth of the steel paddle rise into the air and water seeps from the chamber into the canal. I wait for him to come over and help but he's immersed in the small print of English canal by-laws.

'Actually, in Middle English 'fun' meant to make a fool of,' I say.

'Huh,' he says. 'You know, your sister took me for a Michelin-starred meal when I went up last month.'

'Donna still too busy to come down?'

'Three-star restaurant it was.'

'Never known anyone with that many deadlines.'

'And she was naughty. Bought us all champagne.'

The water sinks and the trunk of an oak downed during recent gales thumps against the gates.

Maybe I have tricked him —the way I've taken to tricking him into conversations at ten in the morning, knowing it's only then when my words will settle at the bottom of his barrelled-brain. Isn't this what we do? Trick our parents in those spaces between the sips? Trick them for as long as it takes to get from Old Hill to The Winding Hole in a battered hire boat with a smoking engine?

He pulls a half bottle of Scotch from his blazer pocket. Then two plastic tumblers. 'Dad, really?'

'I always thought you were more fun than this.'

'But disposable cups. Can't we wait?'

"Dour' her Tom describes you as. *Dour.*'

'That loser?'

'Always angry.'

I hold out my tumbler for him to pour. The lock is still emptying. Trying to force the gates open before they're ready would be a total waste of effort. We finish our drinks and climb back aboard. We steer the boat into the lock chamber and Dad refreshes our tumblers, making toast after toast as we rise amongst the jetsam.

Summer's Gone

When I pull in through the cemetery entrance the road loops and it reminds me of that campsite in north France, of how we had to drive to our pitch real slow because the roads were full of kids chasing beach balls into the skimpy pines and the windows were down, the French heat pouring into our beat-up Jag, Dad turning the music up high—the Beach Boys! remember?—we were all harmonising, maybe the only time in the history of our family we got it right, when the Rhondas and Barbara Anns were still only lyrics at the back of Dad's throat, and I'm still humming *Surfin' USA* when I park up and a woman with a name badge—Deirdre—appears clutching a clipboard with photos of trees, asks if I want a sapling or established, says how some people don't like the old trees because other ashes are scattered there, how I might like a newly planted spot to start afresh, and I think of how we didn't laugh that much together but this would be one of those times we would, and I say no I think we're past fresh starts and I follow Deirdre to a silver birch and she shows me the tree, like an estate agent: here's the canopy, light and airy and the trunk has character although the roots are a bit lived in, and I think, that's a nice tree, you'll like it here, so I say yes, I'll take it, then I see a square hole dug out between the roots and this will make you laugh, I actually ask her, what's the hole for? and I'm not kidding, Mum, I was still expecting that French guy in the golf buggy to rock up and show us how to pitch our tent.

When To Let Go

My ex leaves a voicemail on day three of my holiday to tell me he's chopped off his finger: how the severed tip slid from the kitchen top into his Converse boot and, oh yeah, welcome to his shit new life.

The hotel bartender pumps cream onto my Piña Colada, asks if I'm waiting for someone. 'No,' I say, 'I *like* being alone.'

'Sure you do,' he says. 'Can I get you anything else for your breakfast?'

The phone pings. Another voicemail. The paramedics have said to put the finger on ice till they come. There's only one ice-cube left in the tray. Was it such a big ask to top up the tray when I took ice-cubes? Have I ever tried balancing a severed finger on top of one fucking ice-cube?

I shake the crushed ice in my glass.

He's been googling, he tells me in voicemail three. If the tip isn't sewn back on within a certain time, the finger will continue to grow. He could end up trailing a ten-foot finger behind him for the rest of his shitty life.

I call him back. 'Micky,' I say, 'I'm in Ibiza. You have a girlfriend.'

'I don't want to hassle her with this kind of stuff,' he says.

'I'm in fucking Ibiza,' I say, 'Moving on.'

He hangs up.

The phone stops pinging once I get to the beach. I figure there's no signal. I throw my towel onto the sand and lie on my front. The woman next to me is scrolling through her phone. So there *is* a signal. *No new messages.* The coast seems to be thronging with couples oiling each other's backs, licking each other's ice-creams, passing cigarettes from bags.

When I get back to my room, there are no missed calls. Why hasn't he rung? I picture him bloodied and prostrate, his finger dangling like a clinger vine through his first floor window, reaching out for help.

I light a cigarette from the pack I vowed to throw away and call him.

'I'm good,' he says, when he eventually picks up. 'Sonia came over and she brought ice.'

'So, the finger's saved?' I ask, groping inside the mini-fridge for something, anything, cold and alcoholic. 'Won't keep growing?'

'God, no!' he says. 'It's already healing.'

Trust the Process

You'll breeze through this MRI scan. Isn't that what your hypnotherapist, Sean, told you? That the seventy minutes inside the tube — the time it takes to jet to Bilbao — will fly. Unlike you, going nowhere; abdomen weighted with what feels like a suicide belt, arms strapped to your sides. So what if it's placebo effect? Sixty pounds a session worth of placebo is mucho placebo. The hospital ceiling slides out of view. You find yourself wondering about etymological links between placebo and placenta, seriously, would you fry and eat a placenta? The radiographer asks through the headphones if you're ready. *Yes*, you say to no one. Sean talked about reptilian brains, lizards. You think of crocodiles. Of how your mother used to buy you sugared donuts if you were brave at the dentist.

#

Be open to new experiences. You are a shaman. You are a shaman lying in your low white cave. The shamen lie still as they journey inwards. The machine starts to thrum and bang. You are so shamanic. You are dead still. You are a mummy in a sarcophagus; a dead still dead body bound in bandages torn from linen, organs removed. What will they find on your liver? *Find a rectangle.* That's what Sean said. Find a rectangle and *breathe*; inhale three up the short side, exhale six down the long. But you can't find a rectangle because you're inside a white fucking *cylinder*. You move your eyes. You can do that.

You are in the hole of a donut. You try to breathe without choking on the white icing sugar.

#

Don't overthink it. If you can block out the phone-in radio show piped through your headphones, ignore that Gary from Swansea knows nothing about eighties music and thinks Kate Bush is Madonna, you'll nail the visualisation you've learnt: you won't stop at the top of conjured marble steps and ask yourself how you're supposed to descend into a room designed to make you feel safe and loved, when moments ago, those steps were outside, leading to a sea where you were set upon a canoe to gaze at an unbroken blue sky. You'll descend those steps, albeit still wet from the canoe, and make it into your room, where your mother, alive now, will hold out her arms, tell you it's going to be fine, and Gary will get his last question right.

Were You Ever There?

I wanted to talk about the time you fetched me from school, read me that legal thing—Mum was divorcing you—and how I wasn't crying with you, I was crying because of the kite, I thought we might take out the kite: you and me; and I wanted to talk about the time I doodled on beermats while you fought with a guy called Reg who'd bought a personalised reg which had REG on it, and you said you didn't give a damn about displays of money, you were going to find a cure for AIDS; and that time I spilt take-out and you raged, went out and didn't come back, and Mum said it was my fault —was it? — and the time you asked out my English teacher at parents' evening and forgot to take down my progress scores —what were they? and the time you kept us waiting in the hotel foyer as you went back down the corridor taking nips of Scotch from mini fridges; the time you came back from Rome wearing plastic rosary beads and married to Mum's best friend; the time you spent your pension pot on a personalised reg; the time you weren't made professor—you hadn't found the cure for anything; the time you made me write to your third wife who left you for her therapist; the time I met your fourth wife who cried in the toilets of a Chinese restaurant because you didn't know when to stop; the time I told her I wanted to talk to you—about the drinking— and she said you were out, but I think you were there. When I made that last call. Were you there?

Elephant

The week we learn our father is dying, we bring our elephants to the ward. No metaphors or flowers, says the nurse. I bin the flowers in a bucket left for umbrellas. We stand on the other side of a green curtain. The elephants stamp their feet. We don't know what to do with them. We wait. I google the word for elephant feet and Google tells me elephants' feet are called elephant feet. It tells me too that elephants have five toes and, would you believe this? I say to my brother who hasn't spoken to me in ten years and ignores me still: elephants aren't flat-footed, they walk on tiptoes. I don't care if your elephants float in silk slippers, says the nurse. You can't bring them in here. I point down the corridor. Another family are leaving a room and dragging a reluctant elephant behind them. It's ears flap and knock a drip. The nurse tuts and scoots in white crocs to deal with them. We take advantage and shove our elephants in front of the curtain and line them around my father's bed. They tiptoe in a circle and entwine trunks. Some people say it's selfish to bring elephants to a dying person's bedside. They are probably right. But you tell me. What *do* you do with an elephant in a hospital?

Fogged Horizons

My leg in plaster. 'Only a soft tissue injury,' you'll smile. *Only.* The gauze will be wrapped by paramedics lowered from a helicopter, then coated with plaster bandage dipped in glacial water pouring down the cliff-face.

It's your idea to climb Reinebringen, the mountain looming over our rented fisherman's cottage. 1,978 stone steps built into the mountainside by Nepalese sherpas who hoisted the stones up muddy trails in the Norwegian wind. I stare up at the mountain and inhale the scent of warm rum from the cup in my hands.

'*You* won't have anything to carry,' you say, 'And it's not *hiking* hiking - it's a staircase in the rock,' you add. Like the figure 1,978 was never mentioned. The July sun chases moss down the mountainside, black patches light up as purple fauna. I contemplate the mountain.

'You remember I'm from Essex?' I ask.

The yellow paintwork of our cabin is saturated with the smell of two centuries of cod and the people who fished the cod. 'I'm not coming,' I say and shift deeper into the sofa's crevice eroded by tides of foreign backsides.

I'm thinking of the sofa as I reach the thirtieth step. The fortieth, the fiftieth. An Australian student passes me, asks if

I've seen the bar. Funny. When I slip, this same guy will be on his way back down and will shout, 'So you found it then?'

An hour of pain as we wait for help, your warm hand clenching mine. 'I'm sorry,' I say. I know how much you wanted to get to the top. Who even hikes in Converse? You don't mention the walking boots you bought for my birthday. Nor do you mention the kayaking trip I bailed on yesterday. The voice of an ex —which one? — inside my head: *You always bail!*

Three days later, we take the one road south to the last inhabited island in Lofoten – Å: the last letter of the Norwegian alphabet, and also meaning 'the last place on earth'. How many cartographers marked their own ends of earths? I think of Land's End in Cornwall. Finisterre in Galicia.

I imagined the earth was flat when I was a child, and when the fighting started, doors slamming, I'd close my eyes and start running to the edge — all the way to the end and over.

We pull over at a graveyard. My crutch sinks into the Arctic mud and you take out your camera. Graves in the Arctic Circle are inscribed not with *Rest in Peace* but *Takk For Alt*. Thanks for everything! Some of the graves are simply inscribed with *Takk*. Dead deadpan.

I watch how you avoid treading on the graves, one eye on them, another on me, checking I'm okay to walk. I envision my crutch going through a Viking skull. You're a Takk For Alt person. No doubt about it. Me? Takk for what? Messing up your dream trip?

We get back in the car and head off. I don't realise when we reach Å because I have my eyes closed. 'The end is nigh', you say as we pass the sticker-splattered place name. Can you read my mind?

We park in a layby beneath a wooden awning draped with a dozen open-mouthed heads of salted monkfish. Kelp undulates in the shallow water. The red-ring springs of a mattress rust in a rockpool.

There's a bakery here that sells cinnamon buns baked in an oven from the 1800s. 'The best cinnamon buns in the world,' says the baker, as she drops them into a paper bag. We sit on a rock and let the buns warm our hands. I'm not right for you. When can I tell you?

We stare into the Arctic mist and see the fins of a dolphin pod dip and disappear in teal waters. It's a beautiful end of the earth. A beautiful ending. But the mists are lifting. Another island. You're pointing. But I've seen it.

I bite into my bun and you brush the cinnamon from my cast. 'I'm so glad nothing's broken,' you say. I unhook my arm from the stupid crutch and loop it around your shoulders. Pull you close and we watch as a whole archipelago appears before us.

The Story You'll Never Tell

That story you'll never tell is the house on the street in every Seventies horror movie you devoured in the blue fug of your best friend's mother's cigarette smoke. The story you cannot tell has shutters and a deck and a swinging For Sale sign.

Do you carry a lot of anger? an acupuncturist will ask, years later. He'll suggest an 'aggressive energy drain' with needles pinned the length of your spine. The anger will come out as bright red blotches, he'll warn.

I hope you've got sunglasses, you'll say.

The story you'll never tell starts with a call about a witness statement you made six months earlier. You recall the slow clack clack clack of an officer typing with two fingers; a full hour it took him to get down two paragraphs. It's a work night and you've got bedtime stories to read, kids in pyjamas waiting to hear about gruffalos and wild things. But the caller is summoning you to the station. Can you identify the person they have in custody? And by the way. The suspect is known to them. Do you have family you might need to protect? An online presence? Anything out there which might help someone identify where you live, where you work, where your kids go to school?

This is when you discover agency, like health, or say, freedom of movement, is something you never consider till it's gone.

The story will snake into your dreams at night and pull you into a room you never knew existed, again and again, and your husband will say, Baby I need to sleep. He'll take his pillow to the sofa downstairs, and you'll shout after him, See? This is how they destroy us!

During the daytime, the story will push up against your ribs while you're standing in line at a check-out and a woman ahead fumbles in her pocket for change, saying 'I just can't.' Because you know how it feels to not be able to add, to put things together, to put your hand in your pocket and do something as fundamental as pull out some coins in something resembling a normal transaction.

You can do no more than describe the frayed blue chair next to an overheated radiator. How your finger found a hole and picked through the foam as some uniformed officer spoke of *witness protection, lack of resources, lessons to be learned*, and all you had was the foam and your finger searching for something solid that was holding you up.

This is a story which is boxed and buried. It will come out in fragments now and again. You'll be sitting in a circle and part of your story will pop open like the lid on the tin of biscuits at the centre of the chairs. A stranger will approach you in the break, holding the tin, say people shouldn't get away with stuff. The stranger will say they are part of a global network of hackers who can help you take down websites, publications, people. Help you take down whole institutions. If you like. You smile at this stranger offering you out-of-date biscuits. You've always found chocolate digestives impossible to resist and thanks all the same, but you're done.

Acknowledgements

Grateful acknowledgement is made to the editors of the following journals and print anthologies in which these stories, or earlier versions of them, first appeared:

Fuel: An Anthology of Prize-winning Flash Fiction (Hershman, T., ed. 2023): 'Double Lives'
Fractured Lit (reprint: originally published by Reflex Fiction): 'Yellow Straw, Red Straw'
Flash Fiction Anthology Five, (AdHoc Fiction, 2022): 'Cold Toast'
Pithead Chapel: 'Hotlines'
Ellipsis Zine: 'Parasitos'
Flash Frog: 'Package Holiday: Monastir, All Inclusive'
Life Safari (Ellipsis Zine, 2021): 'Perpetual War: 1983'
National Flash Fiction Day NZ Micro Madness: 'Wall Space'
Ellipsis Zine: 'To His Naked Eye'
Flash Fiction Anthology Five, (Ad Hoc Fiction, 2022): 'Raw Dough Rising'
New Flash Fiction Review: 'Electric Storm'
Flash Flood Journal: 'Red Books'
Bath Flash Fiction Volume 8 (Ad Hoc Fiction, 2023): 'Stress'
New Flash Fiction Review: 'Roaring Twenties'
Ellipsis Zine: 'While My Guitar Gently Weeps'
Bath Flash Fiction Volume 6 (Ad Hoc Fiction, 2021): 'The Last Message'
Flash Flood Journal: 'Wine-tasting for Beginners'
Ellipsis Zine: 'Girls Night Out'
The Phare: 'Undertow'

Bath Flash Fiction Volume 7 (Ad Hoc Fiction, 2022): 'Summer's Gone'
Reflex Fiction: 'When To Let Go'
Centaur Lit: 'Trust the Process'
Scratching the Sands: NFFD Anthology 2023: 'Were You Ever There?'
Bending Genres: 'Elephant'
Stanchion Magazine: 'Fogged Horizons'
Fractured Lit: 'The Story You'll Never Tell'

Immense gratitude to Emily and Alice Mara for their enormous generosity in allowing me to use as cover art 'Portrait of Astrid, 1973' by their late father, the renowned artist Tim Mara, who I had the privilege of meeting in the nineties.

Special thanks also go to the following people: the wonderful Farhana Shaikh for accepting my manuscript and putting it out into the world; Lindz McLeod for initial support in querying; Jo Gatford, Patricia Q Bidar, Sara Hills, and Jude Higgins for generously giving your time to blurb my book and all the various forms of support each of you have given me over the past few years; to Claire Williamson, and to my writing circle 'The Flash Corral' (Suzanne, Ali, James, Sara, Carrie, Emily, Ros, and Anika). To my dear friends, Polly Eadie, for your unwavering support in all things, and Helen Cusack O'Keeffe, who encouraged me to write in the first place. And, of course, to Manuel, Carlos, and Poppy.

About the Author

Kathryn Aldridge-Morris' short form fiction and essays have been published widely in print and online literary journals, including the Aesthetica Creative Writing Annual, Pithead Chapel, Fractured Lit, The Four Faced Liar, Stanchion Magazine, New Flash Fiction Review, Leon Literary Review and Paris Lit Up, as well as being anthologised in over twenty print anthologies and broadcast on BBC Radio Sounds. She has won the Bath Flash Fiction Award, The Forge Literary Magazine's Flash Nonfiction competition, the Manchester Writing School QuietManDave Prize, and Welsh publisher Lucent Dreaming's Flash Fiction contest, and her work has been nominated for Best of the Net, Best Small Fictions and the Pushcart Prize. She is the recipient of an Arts Council England Award to write a novella.

About the Artist

Tim Mara (1948 – 1997) was an Irish printmaker, and his work has been likened to the pop-art movements of the 1970s, although the artist saw his work more in terms of "old masters in modern dress", more similar to Velázquez and Vermeer, by whom he was much influenced. He adopted features of the Dutch Masters, such as light, clarity and stillness, while exploring other themes such as repeating patterns, reflection, refraction and shadow. He liked to look at familiar objects in familiar ways, without iconising them; many everyday objects are printed and juxtaposed in his prints, driving this point home, but also exploring other topical issues, such as the miner's strike, symbolism and identity.

As an artist Tim Mara was unusual in that he worked almost exclusively in the medium of print. Mara was particularly interested in photographic screen printing. This was a handcrafted, labour-intensive process that took up to three months to produce one print. He also used Intaglio techniques in an innovative and experimental manner. In the early 1990s at the Royal College of Art, Tim Mara began to develop a use of colour separation photolithography. He produced several prints between 1993 and 1997 which were either purely lithographic based or combined lithography with silkscreen printing.

Cover art: Portrait of Astrid, 1973
A woman sitting still, by the light of the window in a cluttered living room watching television. The composition is repeated:

Vermeer's 'Girl reading letter at an open window' (1657) is seen on the wall and it too depicts a woman standing by a lattice window; outside another woman can be seen by the window of an adjacent building. The Dutch Masters' themes of stillness, clarity and light are evident. There are many relationships going on in this print: the paperweight and the snowstorm; the newspaper says 'photo-finish adds up to right answer', while the runners' shirts depict a calculation '163 + 815 ÷ 6 = 163'; 163 is also the visible number on the tape measure which is on the cabinet. Astrid was a local girl and her clothes are very indicative of the print's era.

Text credit: VADS.ac.uk